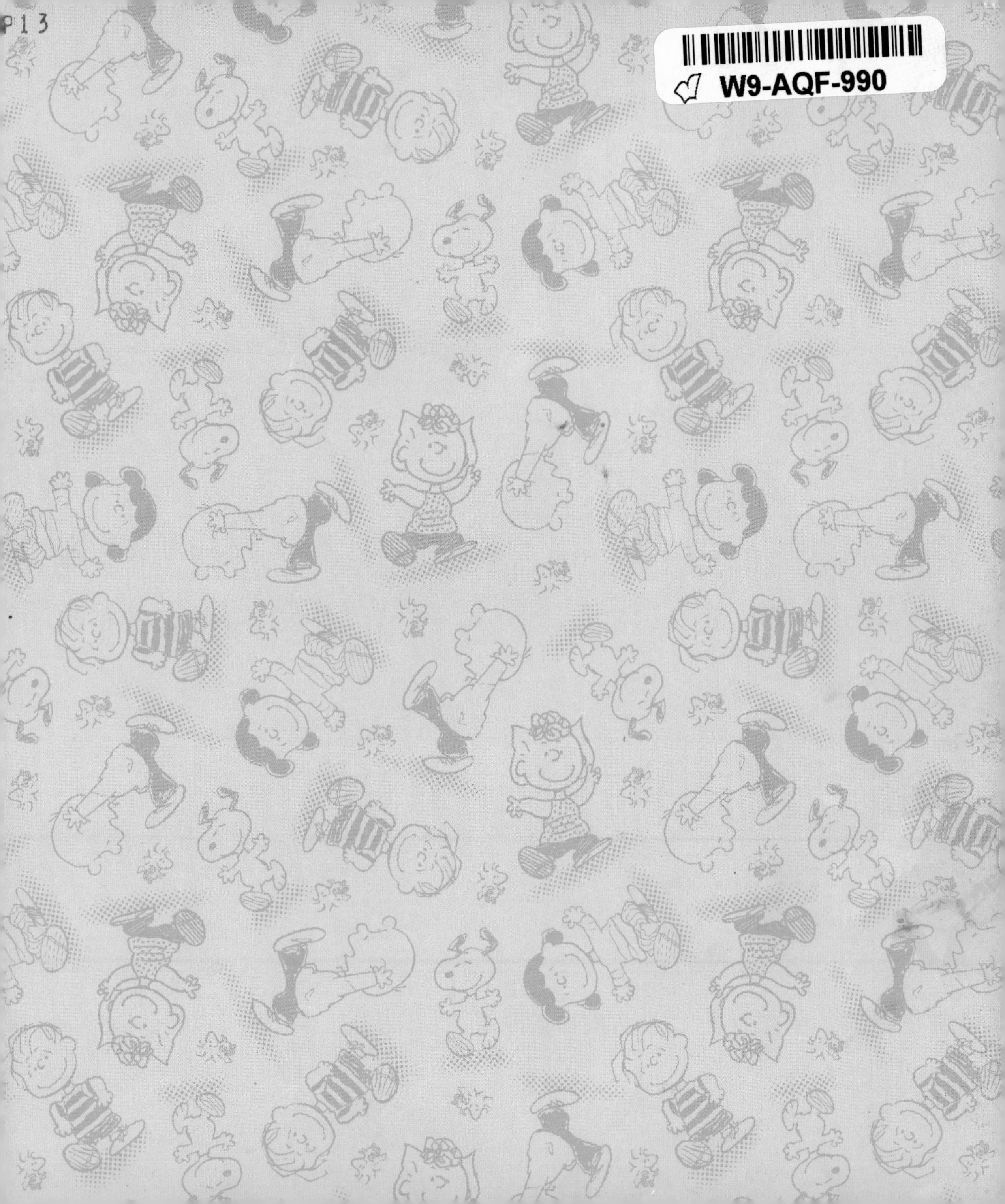

BE YOURSELF!

BE YOURSELF!

Based on the comic strip, PEANUTS,
by Charles M. Schulz

RP|KIDS
PHILADELPHIA • LONDON

© 2013 by Peanuts Worldwide LLC

All rights reserved under the Pan-American and International Copyright Conventions

Printed in China

This book may not be reproduced in whole or in part, in any form or by any means, electronic or mechanical, including photocopying, recording, or by any information storage and retrieval system now known or hereafter invented, without written permission from the publisher.

Books published by Running Press are available at special discounts for bulk purchases in the United States by corporations, institutions, and other organizations. For more information, please contact the Special Markets Department at the Perseus Books Group, 2300 Chestnut Street, Suite 200, Philadelphia, PA 19103, or call (800) 810-4145, ext. 5000, or e-mail special.markets@perseusbooks.com.

ISBN 978-0-7624-4718-3

Library of Congress Control Number: 2012951192

9 8 7 6 5 4 3 2 1
Digit on the right indicates the number of this printing

Art Adapted by Tom Brannon
Designed by Frances J. Soo Ping Chow and Susan Van Horn
Edited by Marlo Scrimizzi
Typography: Agenda and Billy

Published by Running Press Kids
An Imprint of Running Press Book Publishers
A Member of the Perseus Books Group
2300 Chestnut Street
Philadelphia, PA 19103–4371

Visit us on the web!
www.runningpress.com/kids
www.snoopy.com

Just like Charlie Brown, Snoopy, Linus, Lucy,
and the WHOLE Peanuts gang, you can be the best
person you can be. Let yourself shine.

BE YOURSELF!

BE A FRIEND

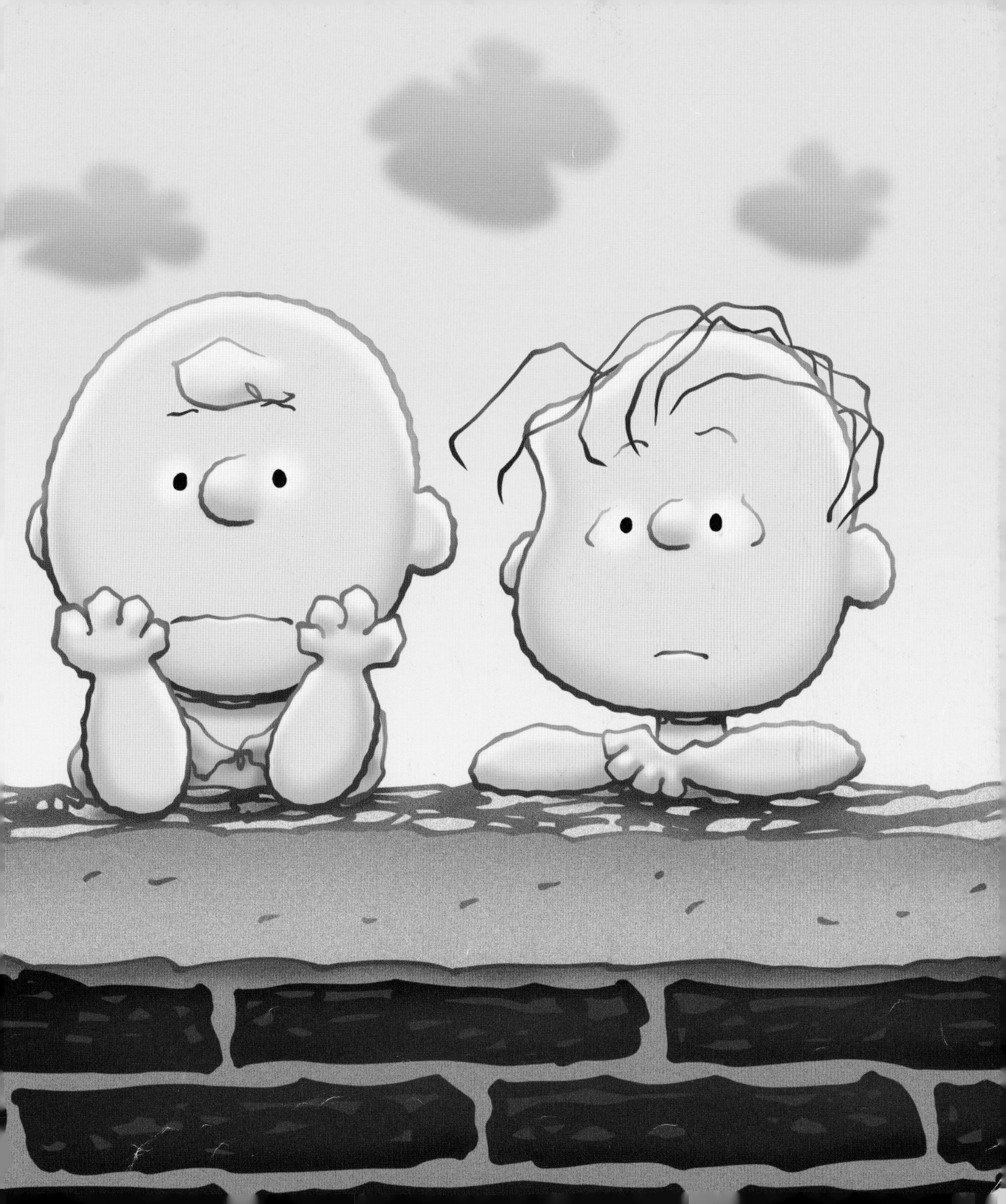

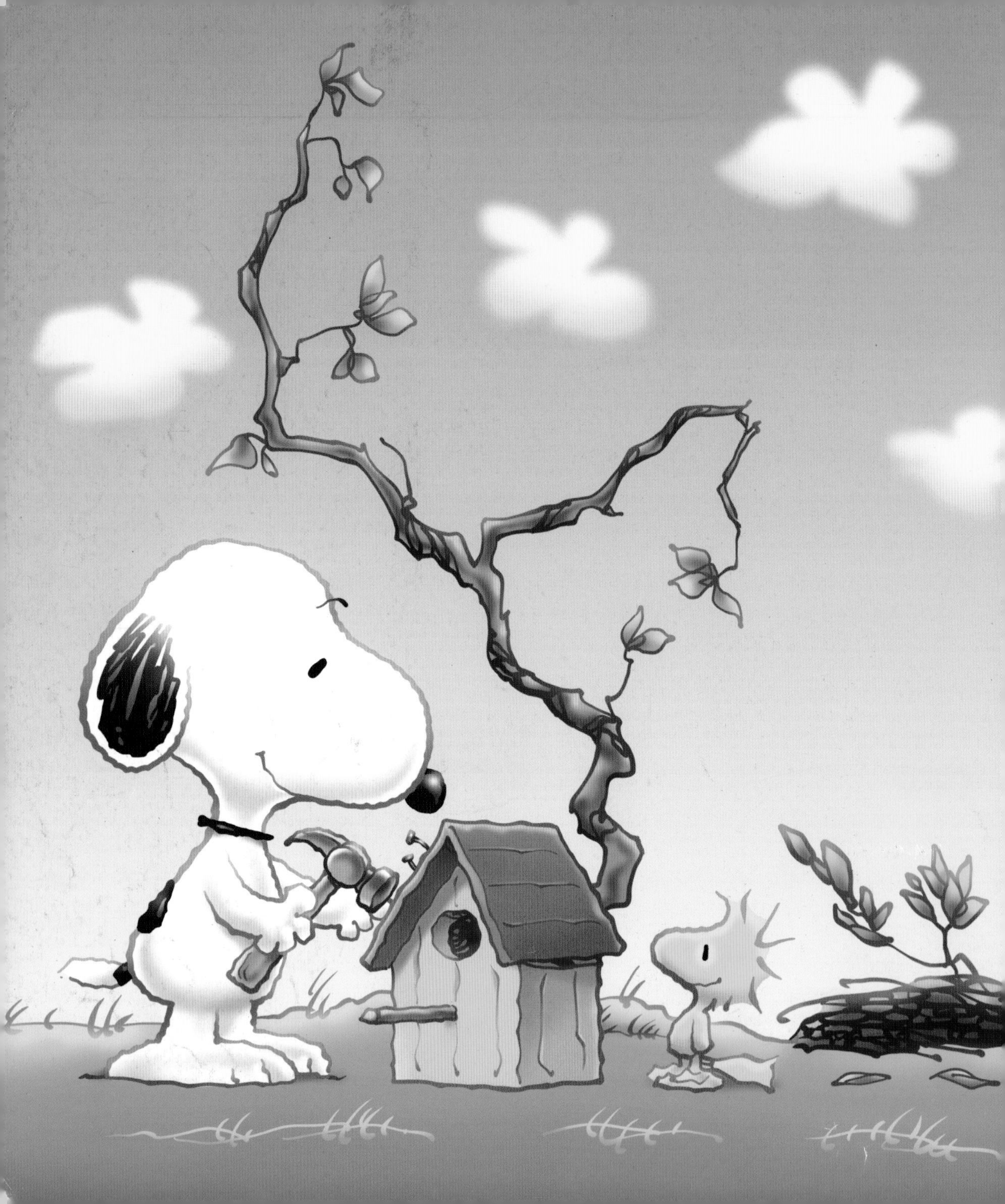

FRIENDS LIKE SNOOPY COME TO THE RESCUE!

Marcie counts on
her friend Peppermint Patty
IN TOUGH SITUATIONS.

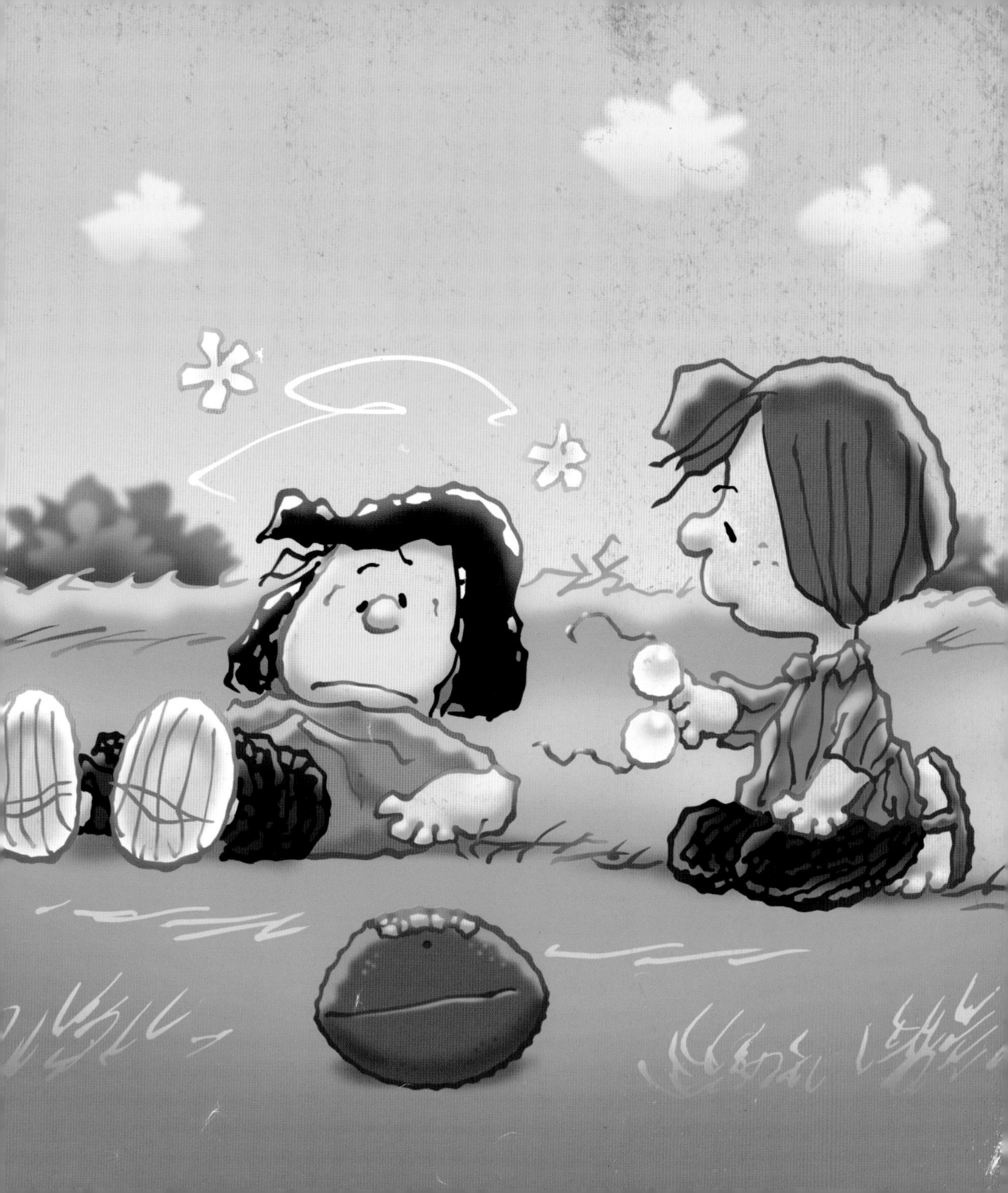

"TO MY SWEET BABBOO"

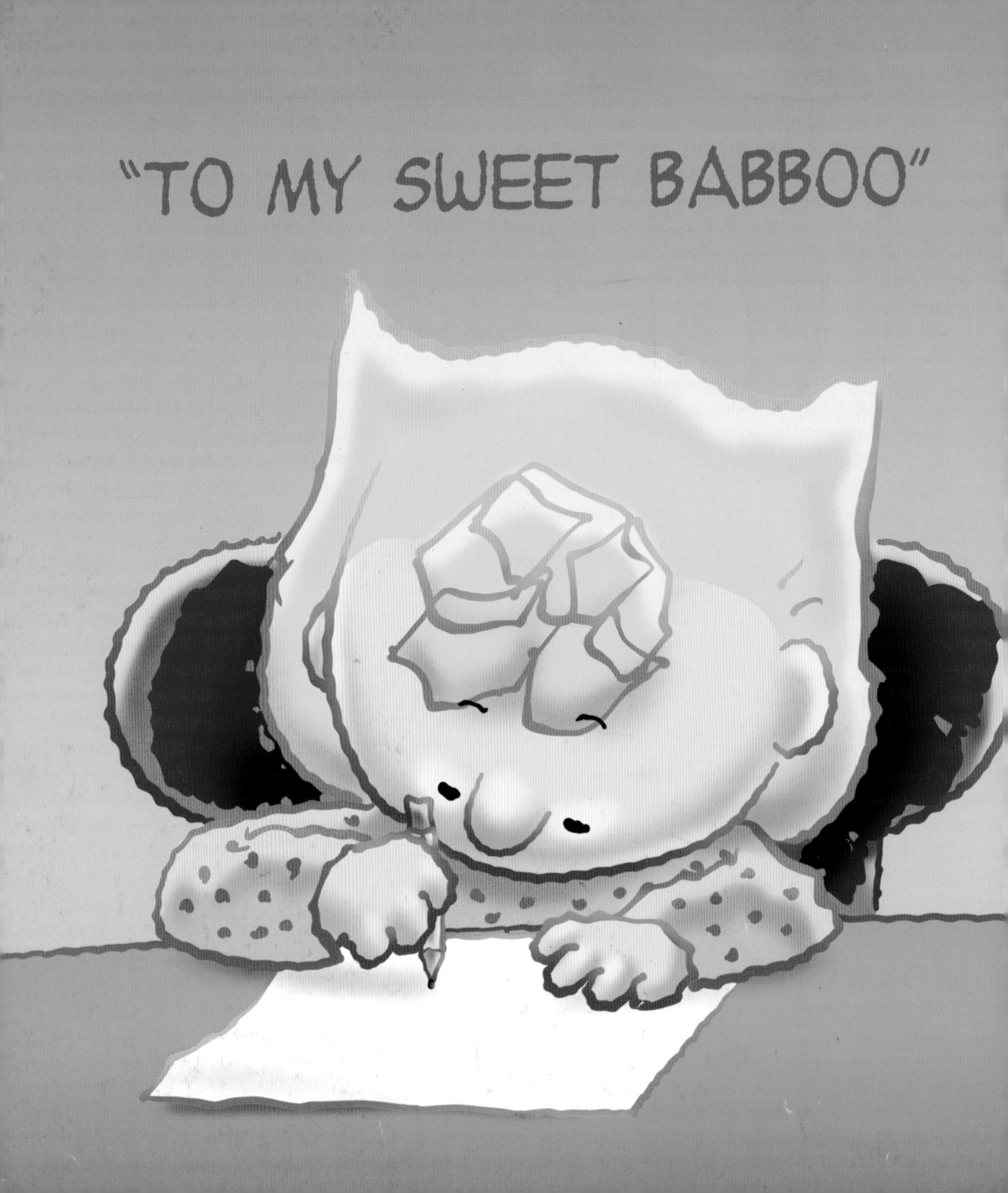

BE LOVING

Lucy is
SCHROEDER'S
#1 FAN.

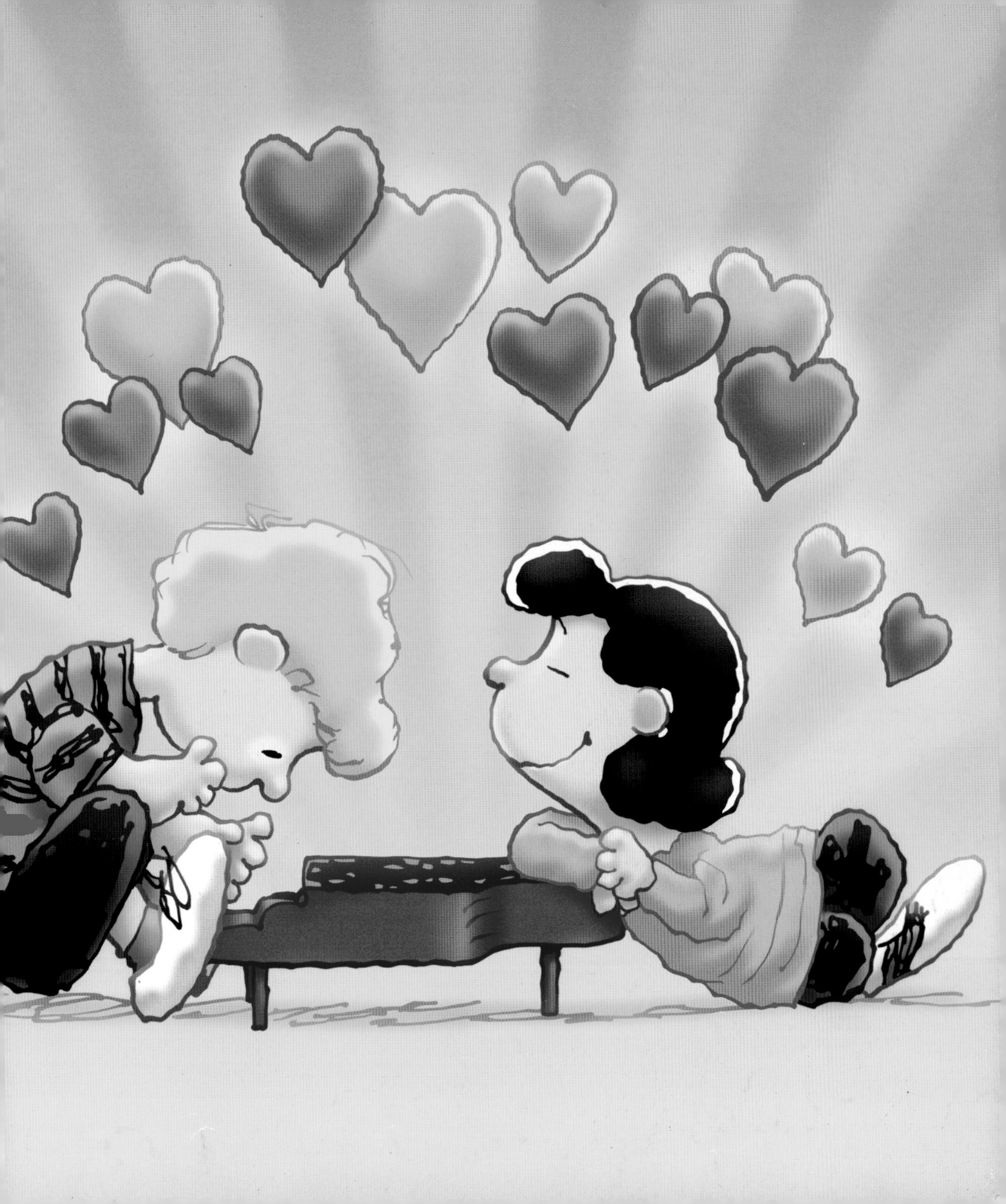

Snoopy the

AFFECTIONATE BEAGLE

is at it again!

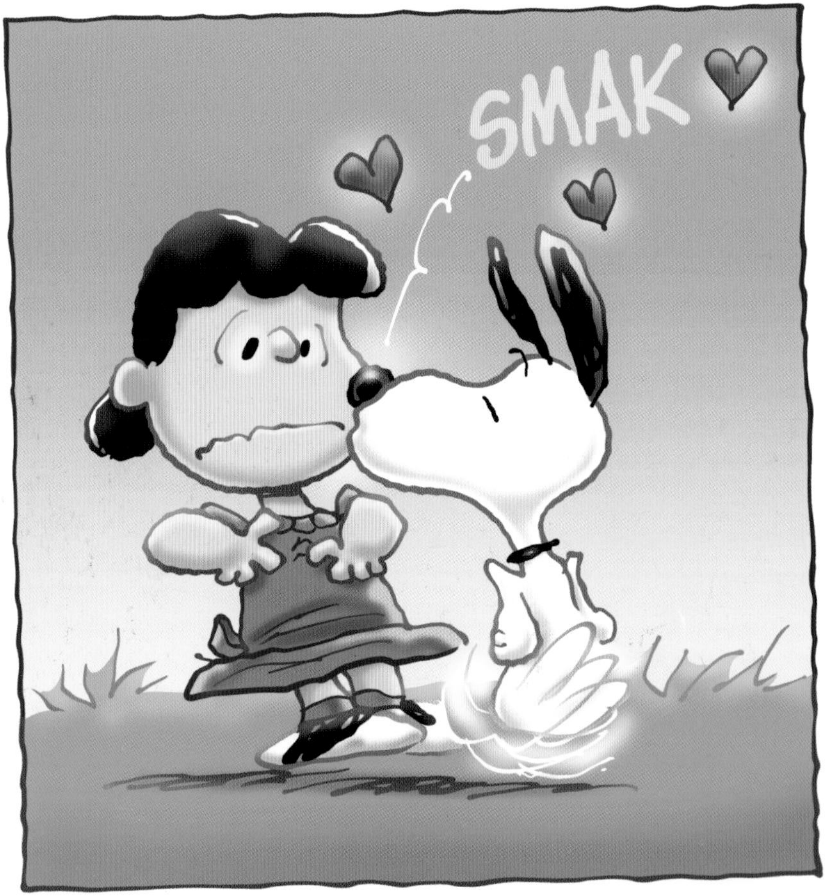
SMAK

SMOOCH!

Snoopy and Charlie Brown
are made for each other.

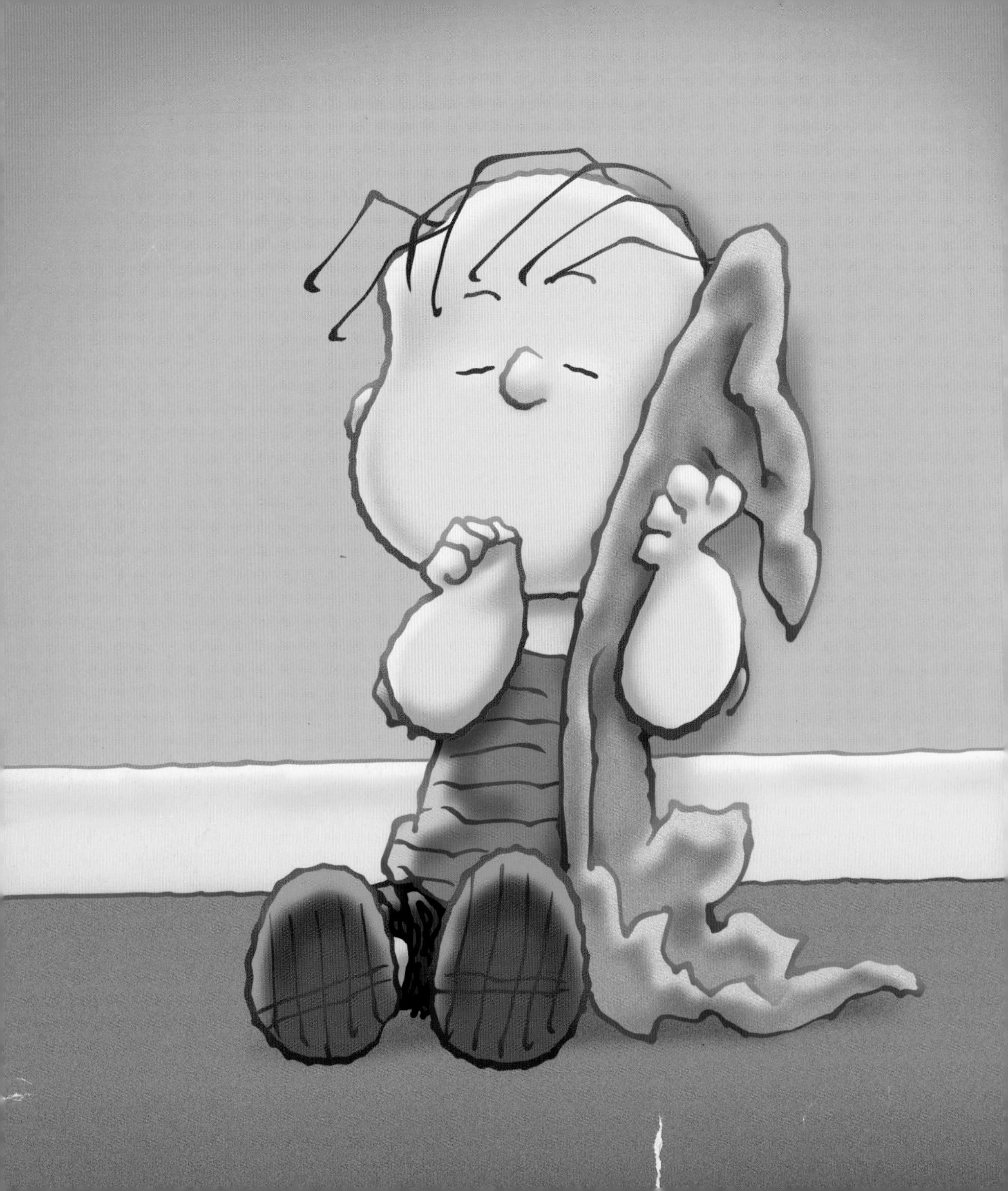

Linus and his blanket:
LOVE AT FIRST SQUEEZE.

BE
DETERMINED

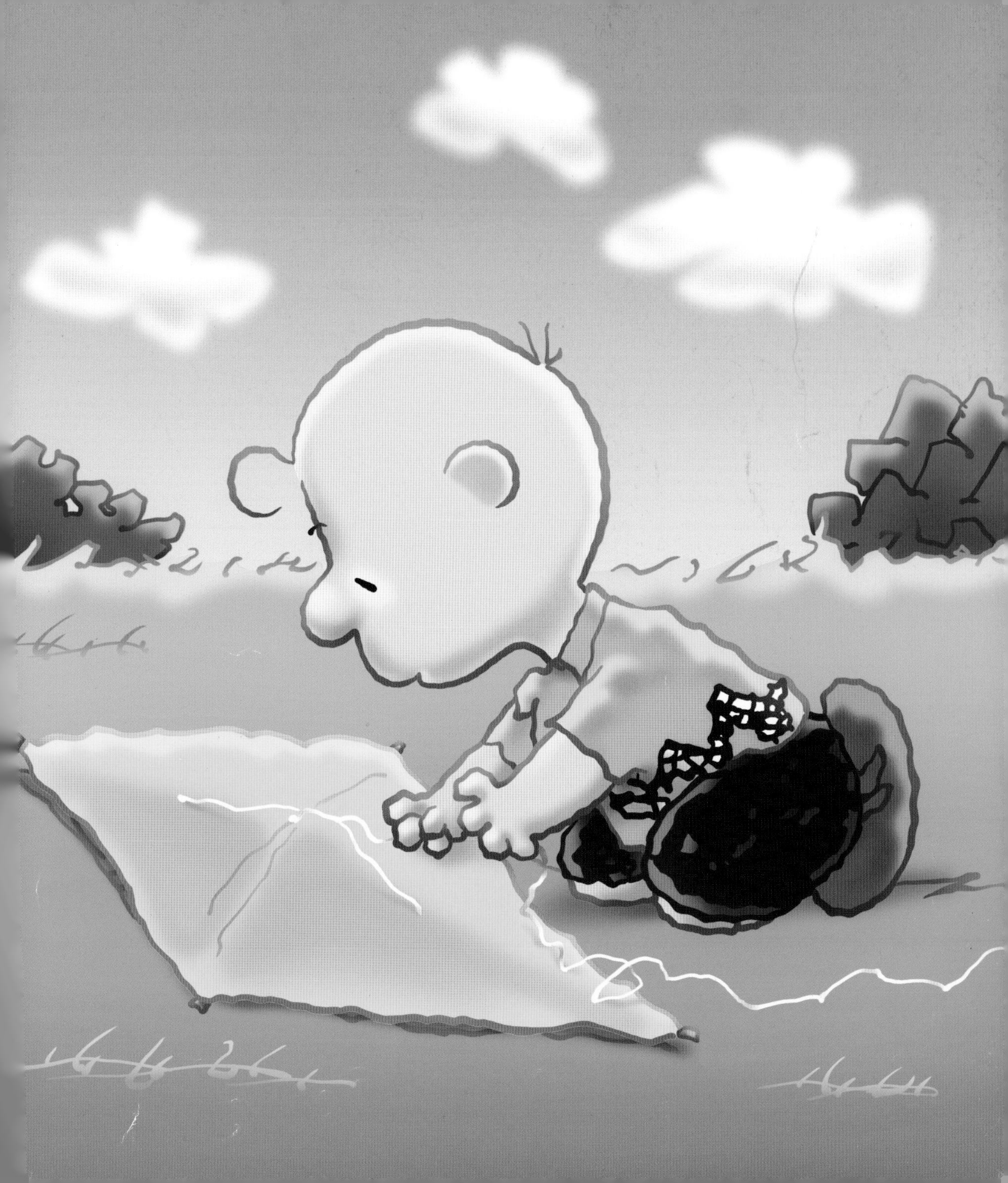

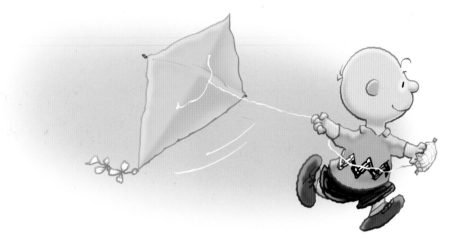

HERE COMES
CHARLIE BROWN....

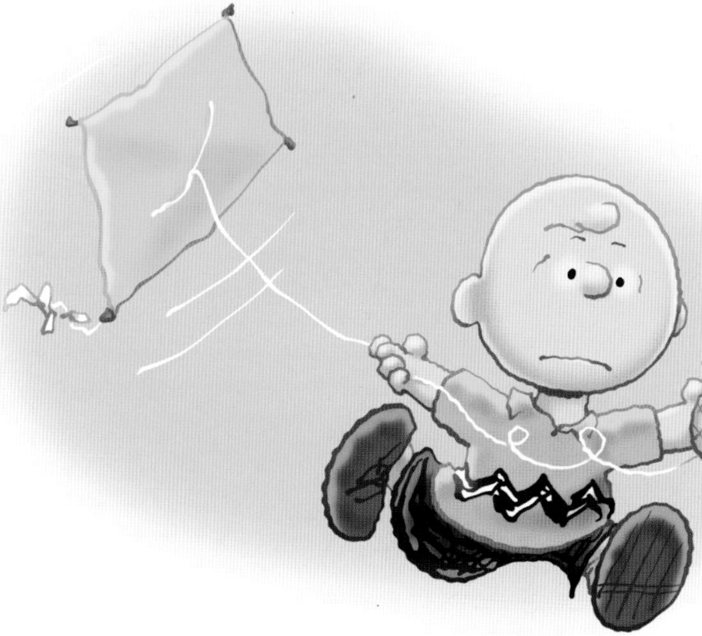

Try again,
Charlie Brown!

Good grief.

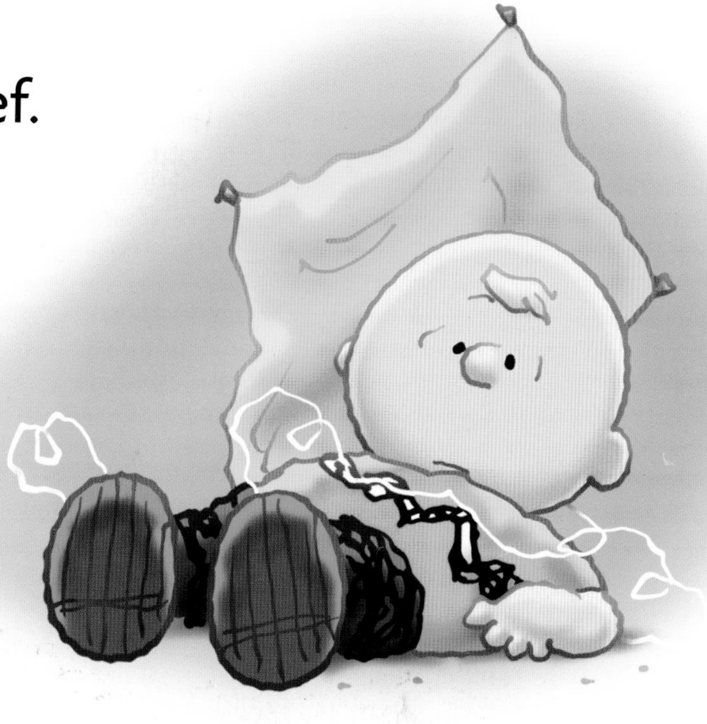

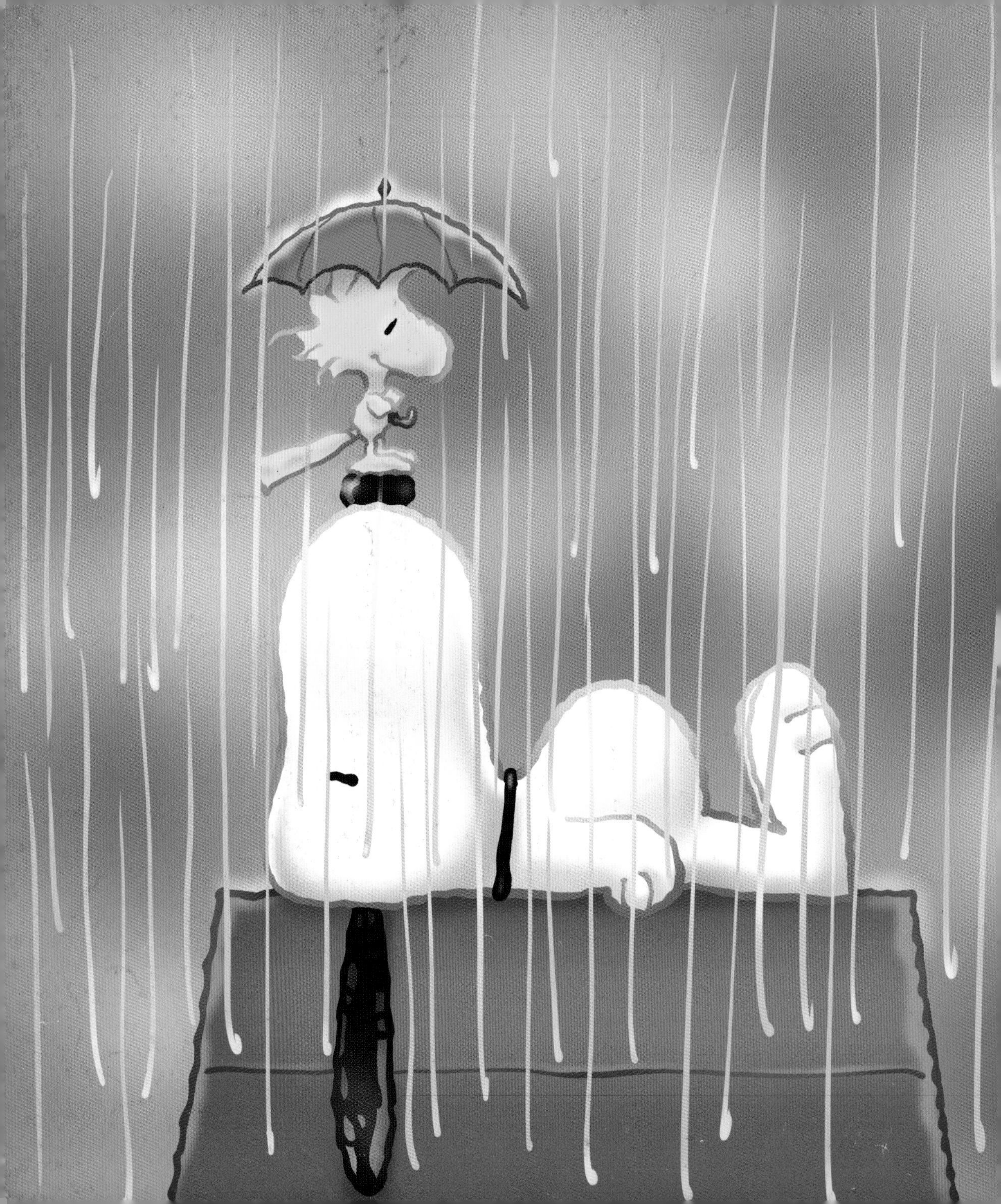

BE
HELPFUL

Lucy the expert can
SOLVE ANY PROBLEM.

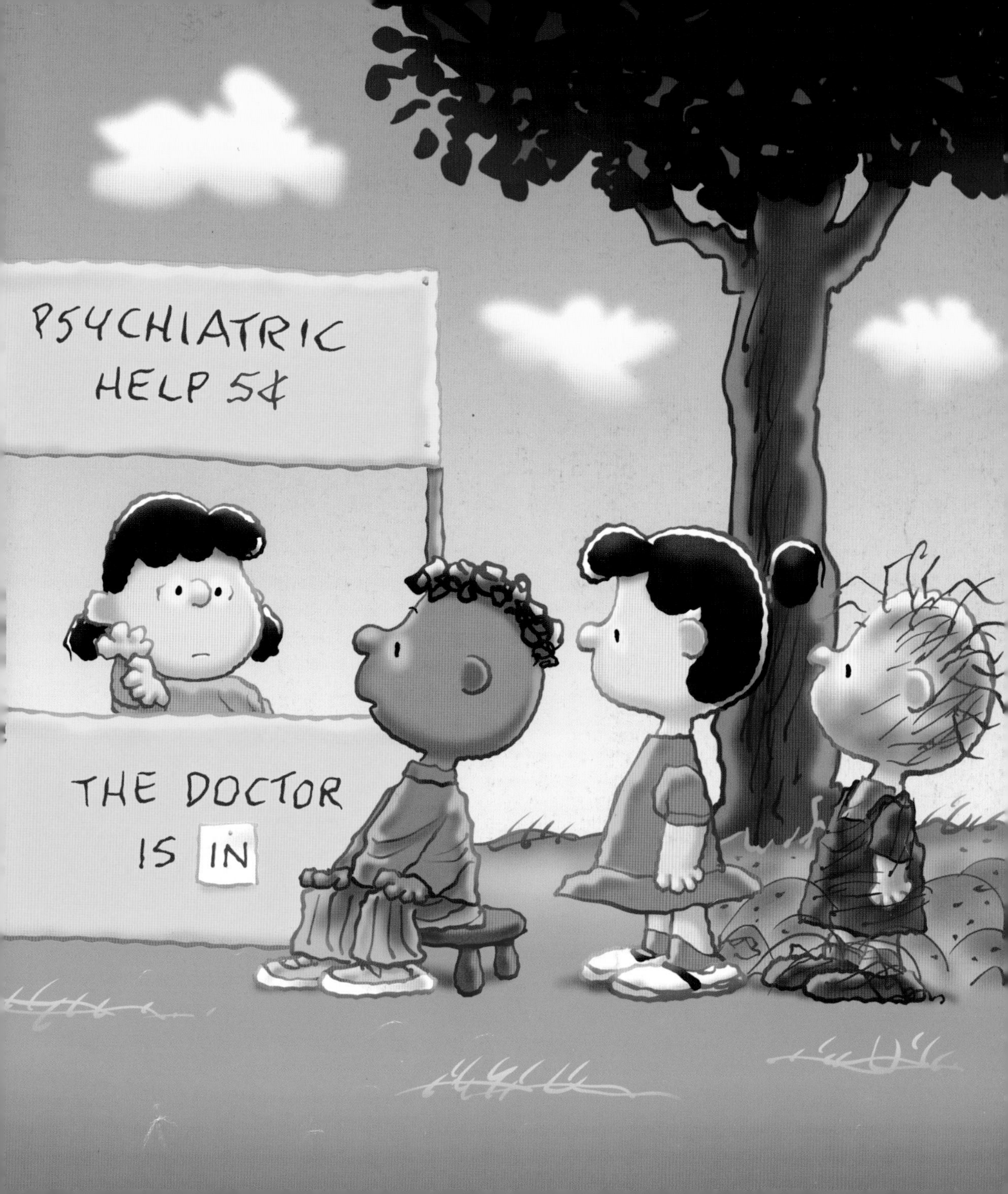
PSYCHIATRIC
HELP 5¢
THE DOCTOR
IS IN

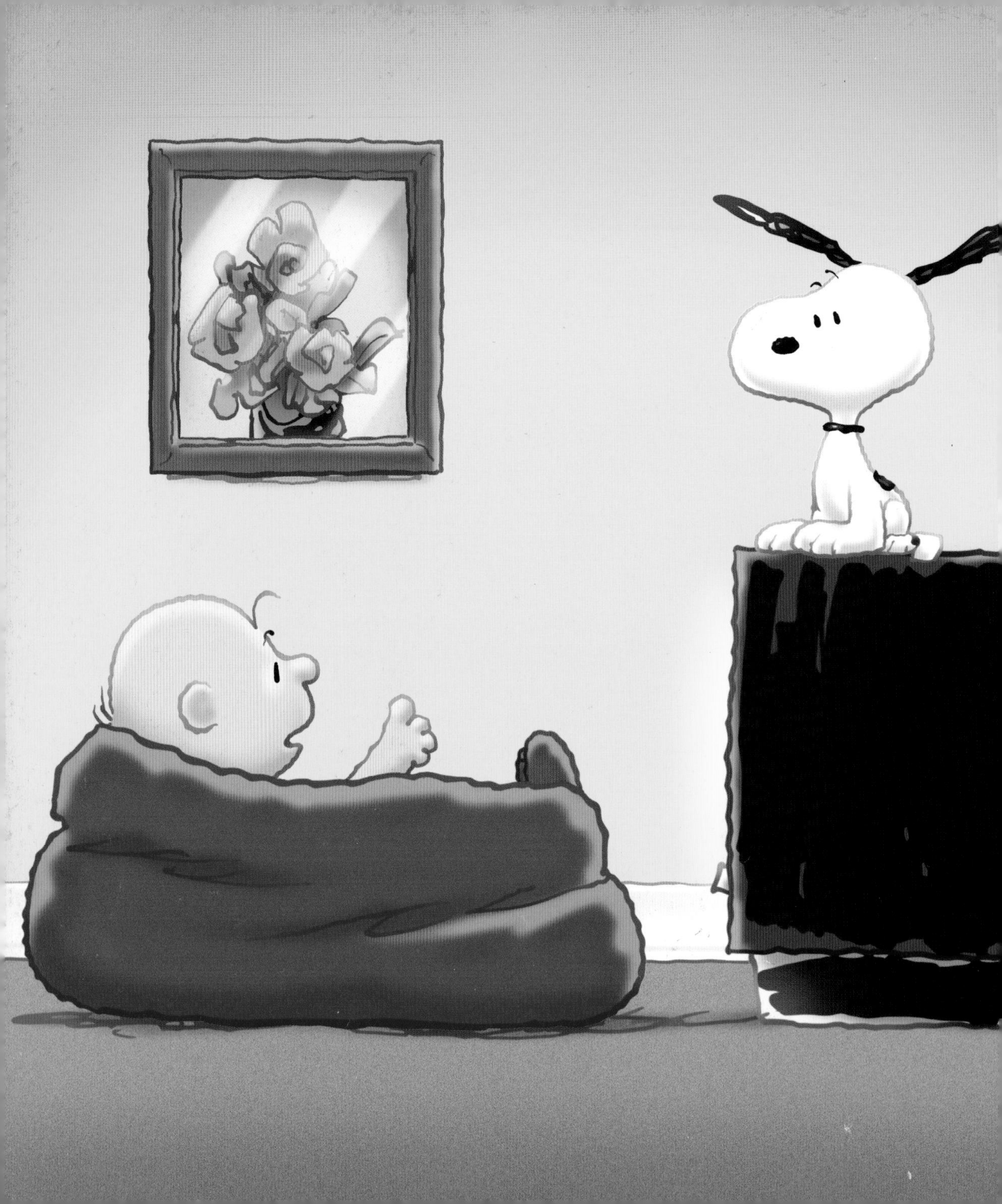

This beagle will always

LEND A HELPING EAR.

BE
ACTIVE

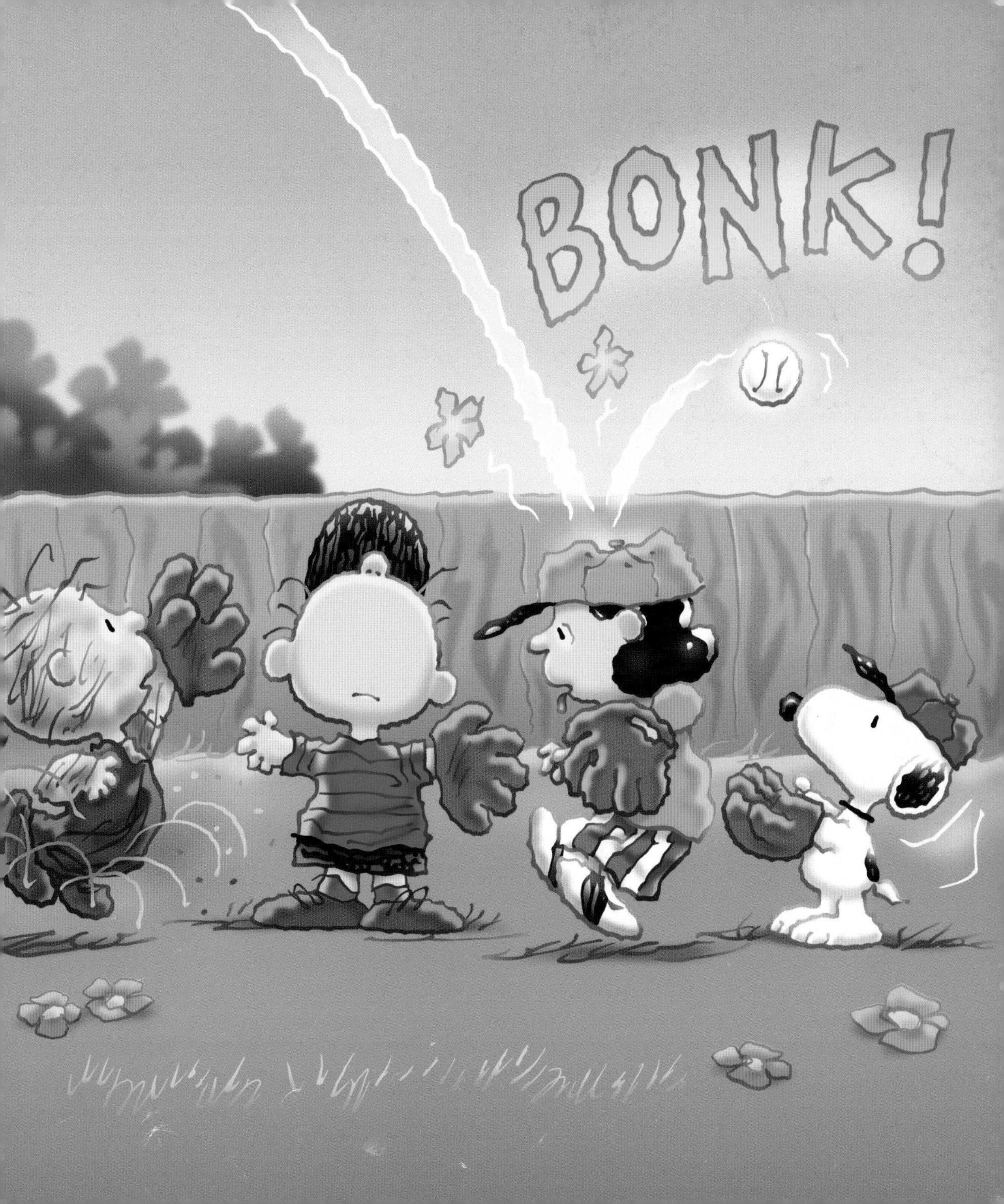
BONK!

Snoopy and Linus
go head to head!

And they're off ...

We have a
WINNER!

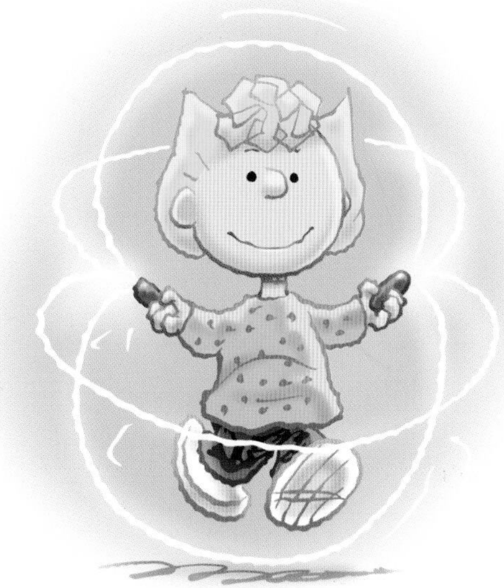

One . . . two . . . three . . .

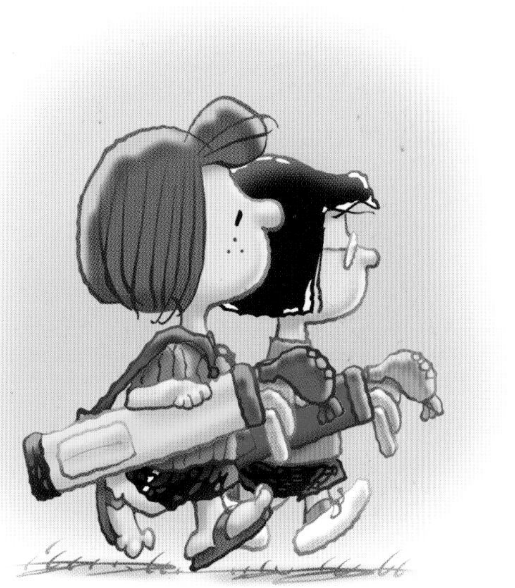

Let's tee off!

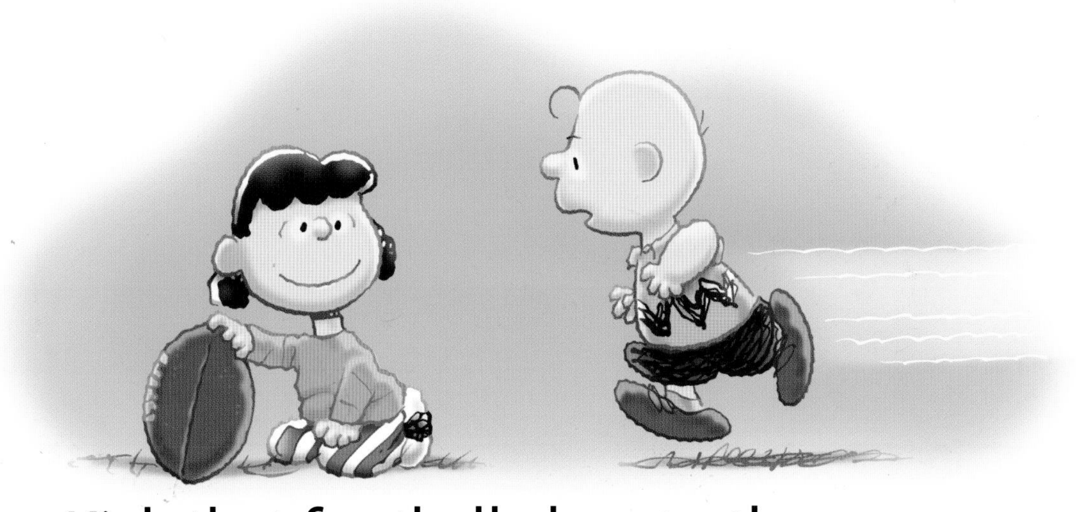

Kick that football clear to the moon, Charlie Brown!

BE
CREATIVE

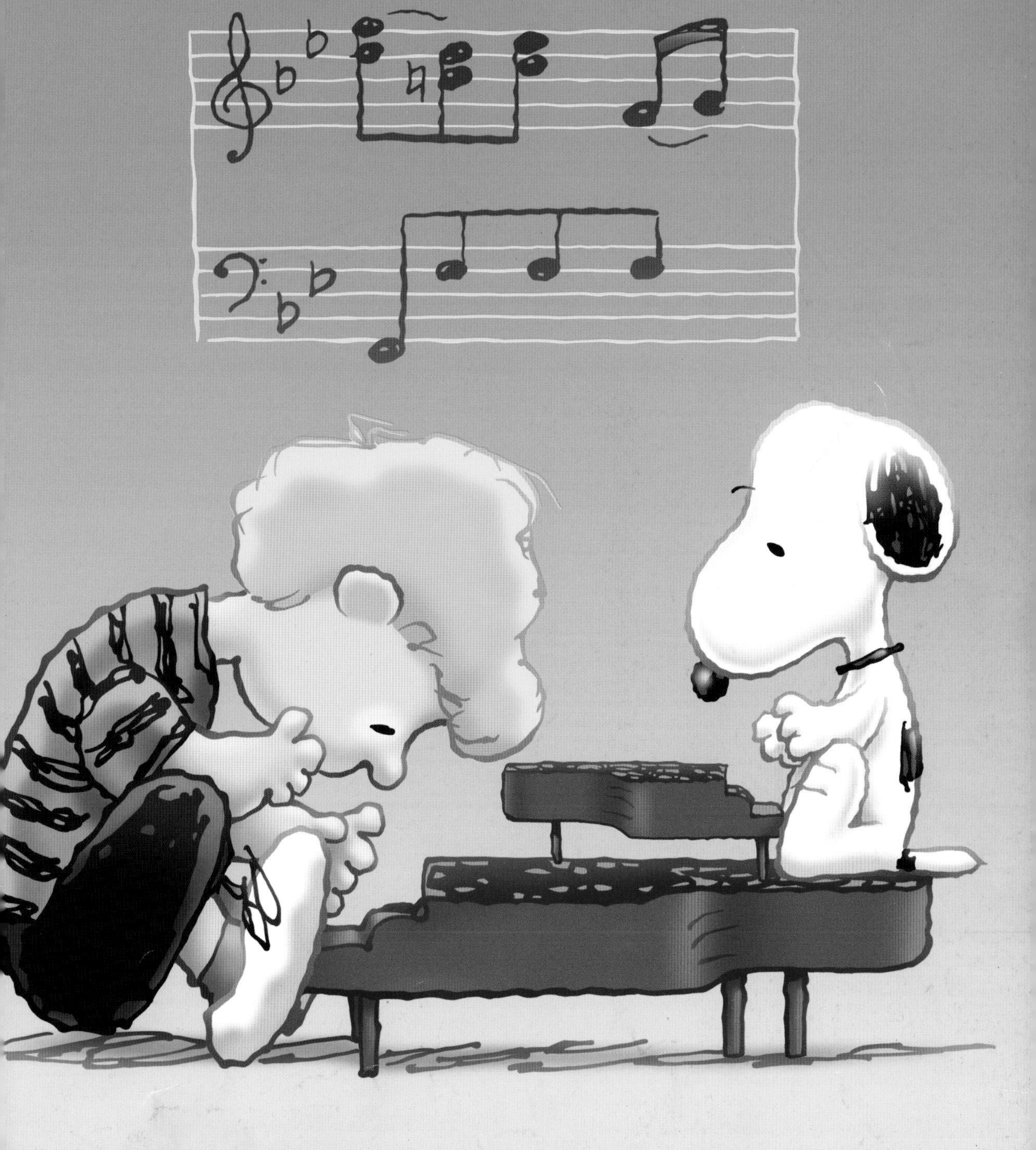

A winning creation is enjoyed by

EVERYONE.

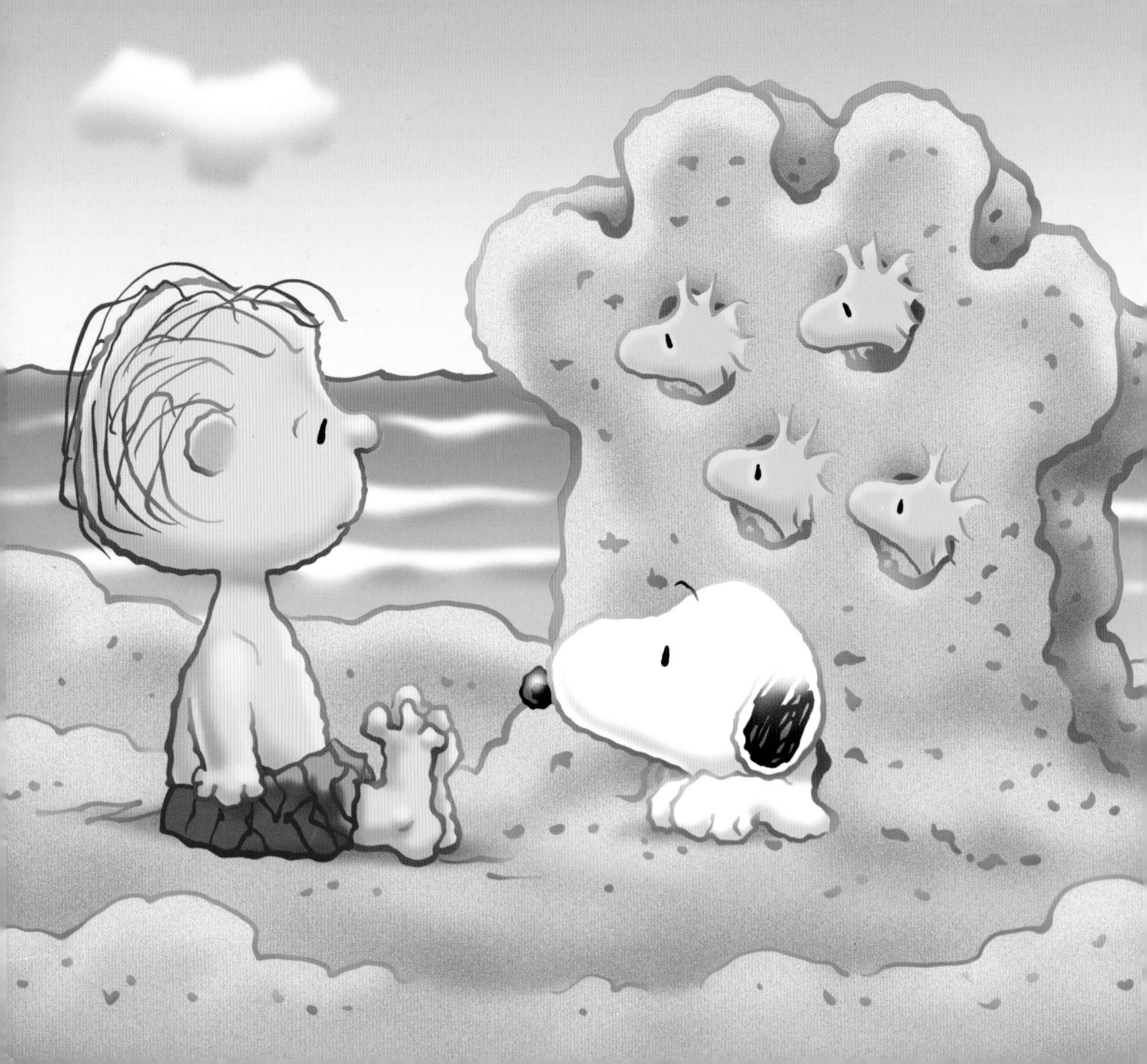

This creative beagle never has

TOO MUCH INSPIRATION.

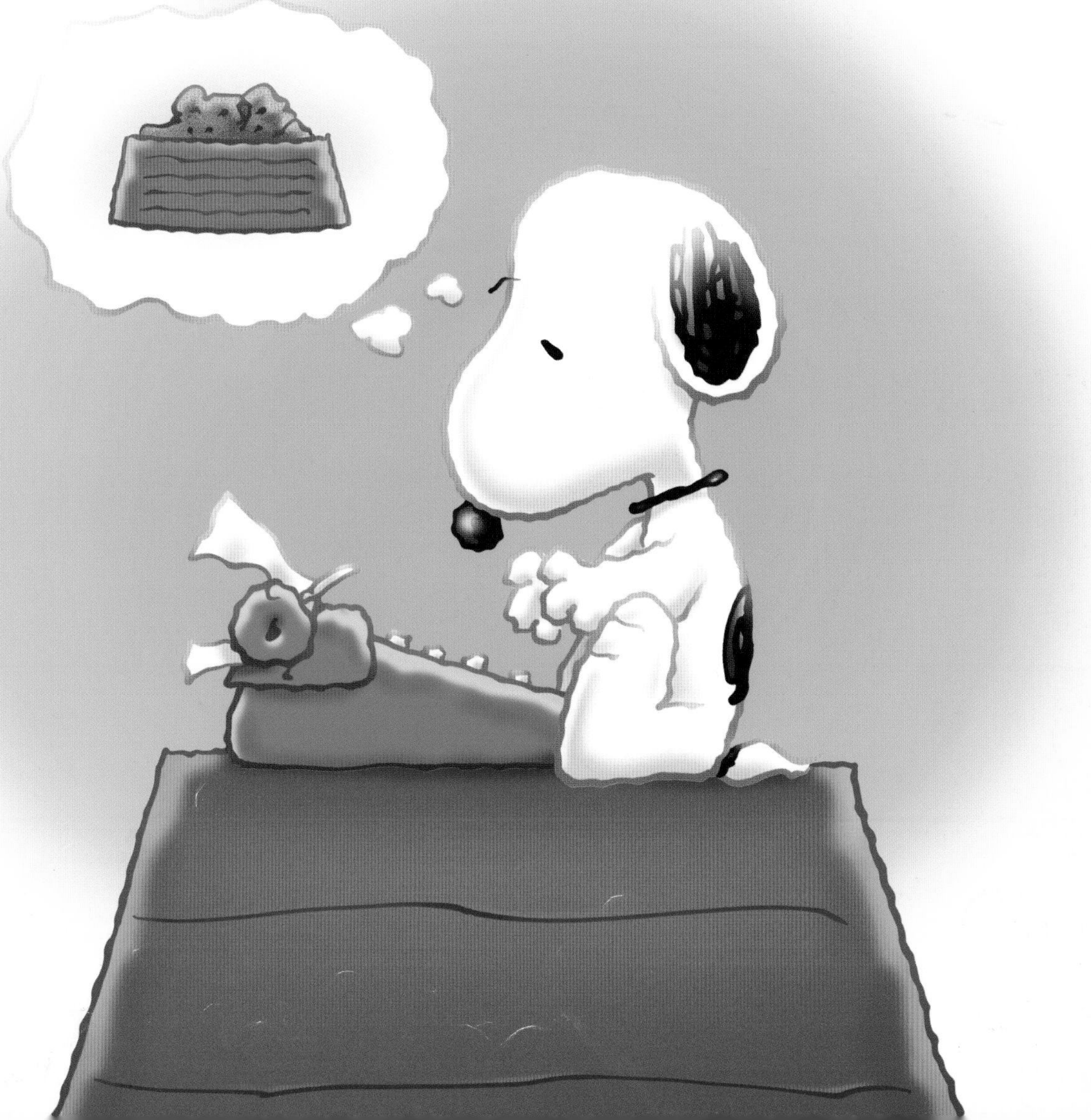

BELIEVE

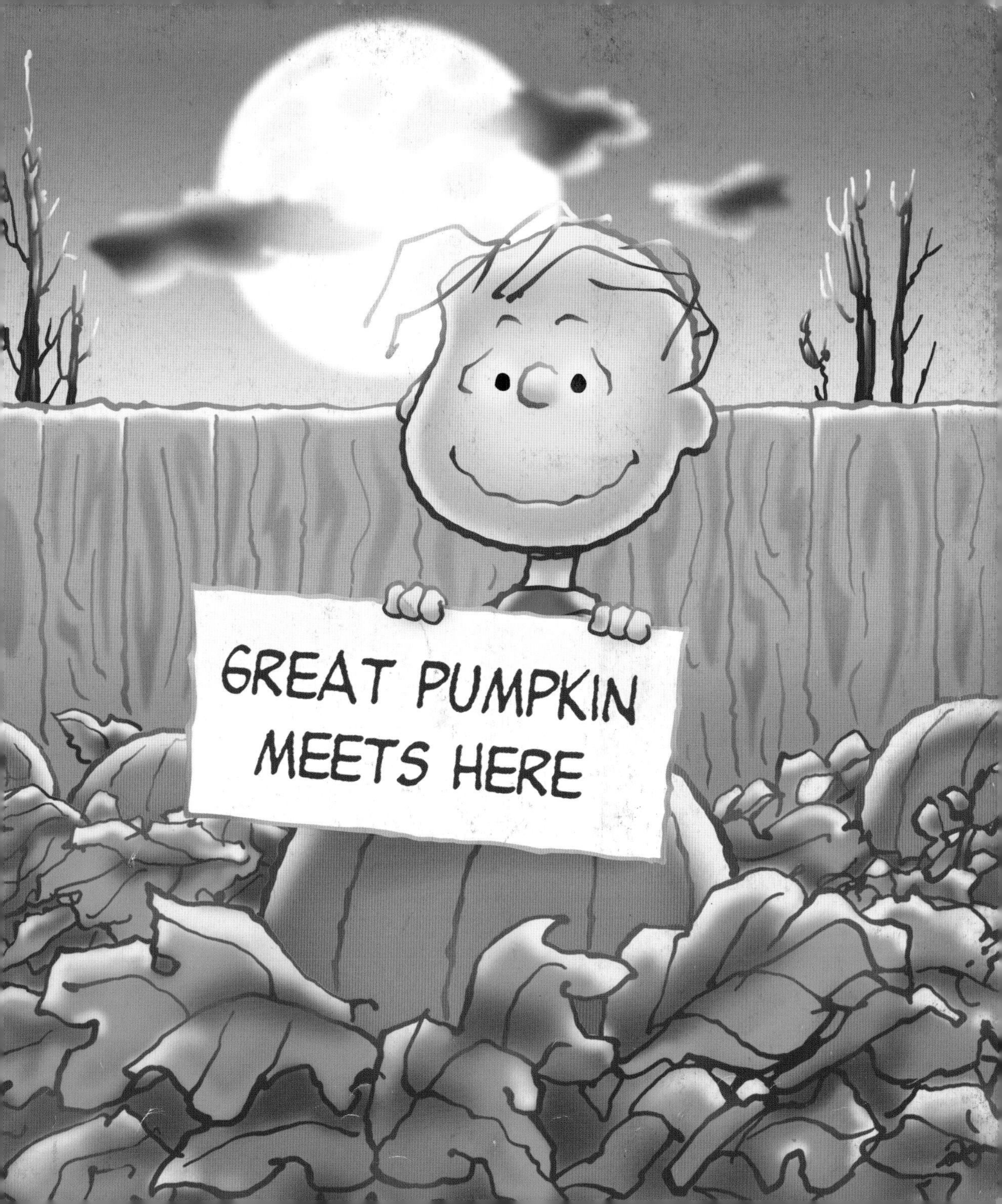
GREAT PUMPKIN
MEETS HERE

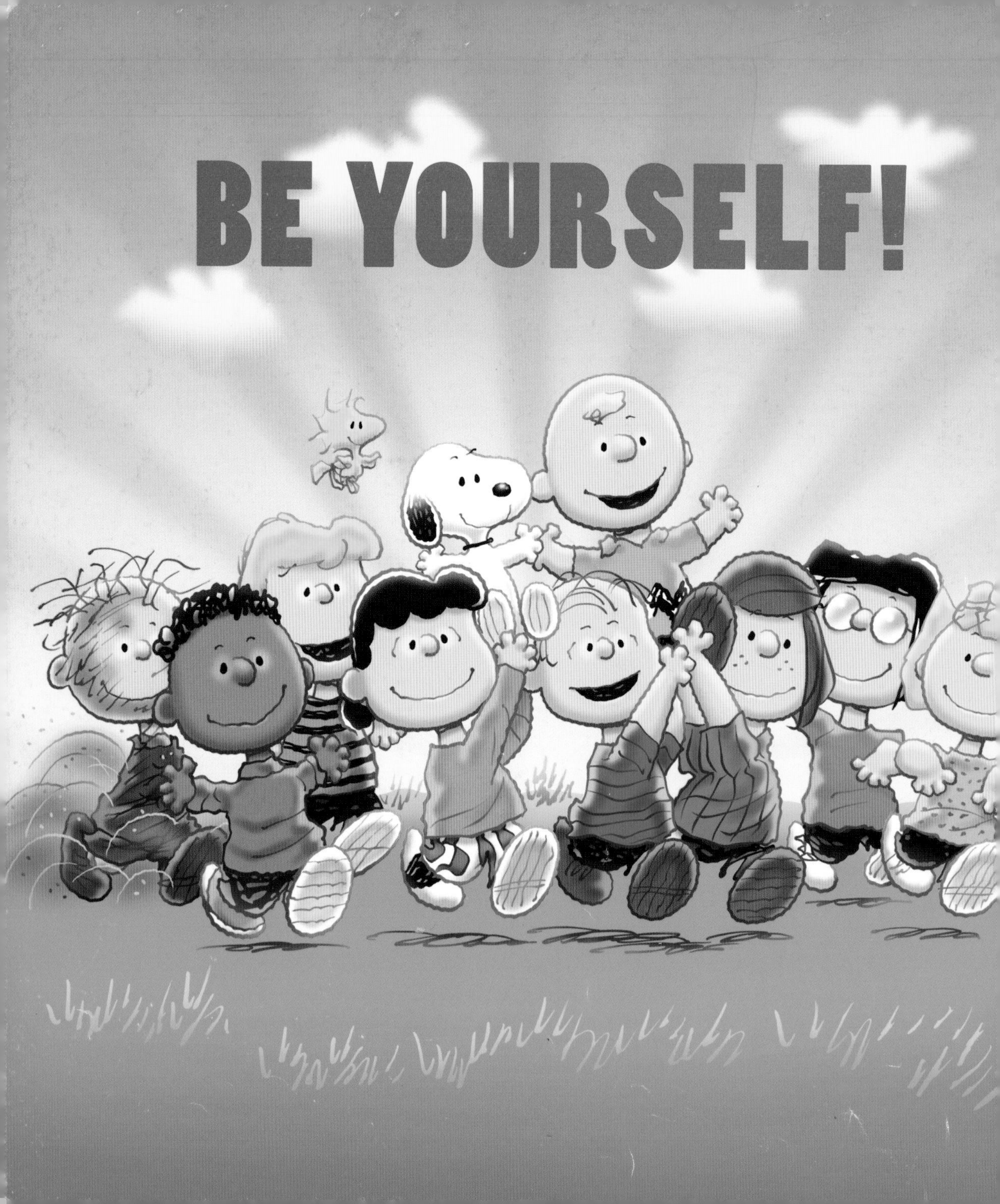
BE YOURSELF!